dan zanes
JUMP UP!

Check for CD in back of book

W9-AHH-361

illustrated by
donald saaf

Megan Tingley Books
LITTLE, BROWN AND COMPANY
New York · Boston

Helen Plum Library
Lombard, IL

E
84.4
ZAN

to alex, anna, isak, lucian, olaf, and piero

Text copyright © 2005 by Dan Zanes
Jump Up! written by Dan Zanes copyright © 2001 by Sister Barbara Music (ASCAP). Lyrics reproduced by permission.
Illustrations copyright © 2005 by Donald Saaf

Going to Boston, Hal-an-tow, Mango Walk, Sail Away Ladies:
All songs traditional arranged by Dan Zanes copyright © 2004 by Sister Barbara Music (ASCAP)
℗ 2003 Festival Five Records, LLC.

All rights reserved.

Little, Brown and Company

Time Warner Book Group
1271 Avenue of the Americas, New York, NY 10020
Visit our Web site at www.lb-kids.com

First Edition

Library of Congress Cataloging-in-Publication Data
Zanes, Dan.
Jump Up! / Dan Zanes; illustrated by Donald Saaf. — 1st ed.
p. cm.
Summary: An illustrated collection of one original and four traditional songs:
"Jump Up!," "Going to Boston," "Hal an Tow," "Mango Walk," and "Sail Away Ladies."
ISBN 0-316-16796-7
1. Children's songs — Texts. [1. songs. 2. Folk songs.] I. Saaf, Donald, ill. II. Title.
PZ8.3.Z325Ju 2005
782.42—dc22
2004013316
10 9 8 7 6 5 4 3 2 1

TWP

Printed in Malaysia

The illustrations for this book were done using collage, acrylic gouache, flashe paint, and colored pencils on Fabiano paper.
The text was set in Franklin Gothic and Adobe Caslon with woodtype dropcaps.
This book was printed on Cyclus offset produced from 100% recycled fibers with 50% post-consumer waste
and 40% post-industrial waste using a chlorine-free bleach process.

Designed by Yolanda Cuomo Design, NYC

3 1502 00621 2284

HELEN PLUM MEMORIAL LIBRARY

3 1502 00621 2284

Dear friends,

when i first began performing music for children and their families, i was quite certain that singing along would be a big part of any show, and i was right. it's a glorious sound when everyone in the room is throwing themselves into a song, and i'm happy to report that it happens all the time.

what i didn't realize when i started on this 21st-century, all-ages folk-musical path was how much everyone loves to dance! it all became clear to me one saturday afternoon when my band and i were playing for a rambunctious group of families here in brooklyn. everyone was clapping and singing with gusto, but when we started playing the leadbelly song "the rock island line" people flew out of their seats and began shaking, hopping, twisting, and waving their limbs in every direction. we played "polly wolly doodle" and "all around the kitchen" and the same thing happened. since that afternoon, whether i've played with my band or by myself, the show always breaks down into a dance party.

"jump up" is a song i wrote while sitting at my kitchen table thinking about dancing with my friends. except for the sound of my guitar, the house was quiet and through the open windows i could hear kids on bikes yelling, church bells ringing, dogs barking, and the occasional car rumbling by. what a lively neighborhood to live in, i thought; who wouldn't want to jump out of bed and dance?

i hope that your days are filled with songs and dances. thank you for the inspiration.

Love, Dan

Jump up, day is breaking

I

know you're lying down

Jump up,

bells are ringing

h yeah, it's a crazy sound

Jump up,

Reach out, grab a rainbow

turn it upside down

Jump up,
     clouds are passing

i know we'll be laughing too

a new day is shining down

jump up, day is breaking
jump up, let's get shaking
i know you're lying down
jump up and we'll dance around

jump up, bells are ringing
and i hear friends are singing
oh yeah, it's a crazy sound
jump up and we'll dance around

jump up, stand on your tip toes
reach out, grab a rainbow
turn it upside down
jump up and we'll dance it around

jump up, clouds are passing
look up, the sky is laughing
i know we'll be laughing too
jump up i want to dance with you

jump up, you know i love you
that's right, i love love love you
a new day is shining down
jump up and we'll dance around!

JUMP UP

years ago my friend ron told me about going to a raucous trinidadian dance. he said that it was called a "jump up." i thought that was a telling name for a musical party, and it never quite left my mind. of course, it makes so much sense. if you're really going to dance, first you have to jump up out of your chair. "stand up" or "rise up" wouldn't convey nearly the same excitement. "jump up" tells the whole story.

when i was trying to write the final song for our family dance cd, the words "jump up" came out of my mouth and the song seemed to compose itself. i like playing it alone, i love playing it with my band, and i'm glad that ron told me about the wild night out with his friends from trinidad.

come on girls, we're going to boston
come on girls, we're going to boston
come on girls, we're going to boston
early in the morning

won't we look pretty in the ballroom
won't we look pretty in the ballroom
won't we look pretty in the ballroom
early in the morning

saddle up boys, let's go with them. . .

won't we look pretty when we're dancing. . .

johnny i'm going to tell your pappy. . .

won't we look pretty in the ballroom. . .

swing your partner all the way to boston. . .

won't we look pretty when we're dancing. . .

swing your partner all the way to boston. . .

won't we look pretty in the ballroom. . .

GOING TO BOSTON

over the years i've found a number of old songbooks in thrift shops and at flea markets. i found "going to boston" in a little paperback called *early american songs*. it sold for 40 cents in 1943. the authors, margaret and travis johnson (a.k.a. the song-spinners), call this song a "long ways dance play-party song."

in the 19th century, the church frowned upon the idea of young people dancing to music. play parties included many of the movements found in square dances, but because the songs were sung without instrumentation (and the events were called play parties rather than dances), they were usually considered acceptable. for a musical walk through some of these songs, pete seeger, along with his daughter mika and the reverend larry eisenberg, recorded *american playparties* for the folkways label.

kentucky–born singer and dulcimer player jean ritchie recorded a soulful version of "going to boston" on her record called *marching across the green grass and other american children game songs*.

H AL-AN-TOW

this is a traditional english song that celebrates the end of winter and the coming of summer. it would take more room than i have here to give the historical background of this song, but it's interesting to note that every year on may 8, Hal-an-Tow is part of the helston (in cornwall) furry day (the feast of saint michael). during the procession people dance through the streets, making noise to drive away the spirits of winter and make room for beautiful weather. dancers snake through the streets, often winding in someone's front door and out the back.

This has been a rousing sing-along song at shows lately. the part of the drum is well suited for hand claps. i love songs that connect me with traditions that relate to the natural world, and who doesn't like to belt out lyrics of the coming spring?

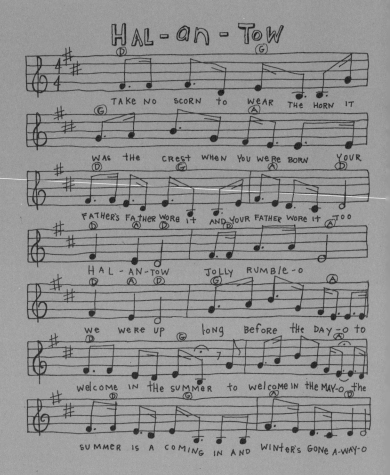

take no scorn to wear the horn
it was the crest when you were born
your father's father wore it
and your father wore it too

hal-an-tow jolly rumble-o
we were up long before the day-o
to welcome in the summer
to welcome in the may-o
for summer is a-coming in
and winter's gone away-o

what happened to the spaniards
that made so great a boast-o?
why they shall eat the feathered goose
and we shall eat the roast-o

hal-an-tow. . .

robin hood and little john
have both gone to the fair-o
and we will to the merry green wood
to hunt the buck and hare-o

hal-an-tow. . .

god bless the merry moses
and all that power and might-o
and send us peace to england
send peace by day and night-o

hal-an-tow. . .
hal-an-tow. . .

your brother did a-tell me that you go mango walk
you go mango walk, you go mango walk
your brother did a-tell me that you go mango walk
and thief up the number 'levens

i'll tell you joe, i'll tell you for true
i'll tell you for true, i tell you
i never went to no mango walk
and thief up the number 'levens

i worry what you're saying, lily love of my heart
lily love of my heart, lily love of my heart
your brother did a-tell me that you go mango walk
and thief up the number 'levens

and you mean to say my drop of sunshine
that you really believe that liar
i never went to no mango walk
and thief up the number 'levens

your brother did a-tell me that you go mango walk
you go mango walk, you go mango walk
your brother did a-tell me that you go mango walk
and thief up the number 'levens

MANGO WALK

i spent four years of my life listening to nothing but jamaican music. the rhythms and the catchy melodies pulled me in, but what kept me interested was the way that everyday life became such a rich subject matter for the different songs. here's a perfect example.

i found this song in a couple of song books, one called *jamaican folk songs*, which was printed for the music mart in kingston, jamaica, and one called *hi ho the rattlin' bog and other folk songs for group singing*, selected by john langstaff. we took ingredients from both versions and came up with this version.

the "number 'levens" in question here are a particular-sized mango. were they stolen? i don't know, but what a good subject for a song. this one gets stuck in my head for days at a time.

SAIL AWAY LADIES

this is an old, southern mountain tune. i've heard it sung and i've heard it played as a dance instrumental. there are many versions of "sail away ladies" loose in the world, and from these i picked my favorite verses. i looked the song over and realized that the boys got all the property. however, these folk songs are flexible; they're living and breathing and they change over time depending on people's needs. with this in mind i wrote a verse for my daughter and gave her a house.

in 1926 a man named "uncle bunt" stephens recorded an untamed fiddle version of this song. it was later included in harry smith's *anthology of american folk music*. if you like to fill the air in your home with the wild and mysterious sounds of handmade music from america's past, i would recommend this collection.

ain't no use to sit and cry
sail away ladies, sail away
you'll be an angel by and by
sail away ladies, sail away

don't she rock 'em die-dee-o,
don't she rock 'em die-dee-o,
don't she rock 'em die-dee-o,
sail away ladies, sail away

ever i get my new house done,
sail away ladies, sail away
give my old one to my son
sail away ladies, sail away

don't she rock 'em die-dee-o. . .

i built my place down by the water
sail away ladies, sail away
give the whole thing to my daughter
sail away ladies, sail away

don't she rock 'em die-dee-o. . .

come along friends and go with me
sail away ladies, sail away
we'll go back to tennessee
sail away ladies, sail away

don't she rock 'em die-dee-o. . .

ain't no use to sit and cry
sail away ladies, sail away
you'll be an angel bye and bye
sail away ladies, sail away

don't she rock 'em die-dee-o. . .

don't she rock 'em die-dee-o. . .